Richard Scarry's
Little
Counting
Book

Random House 🏠 New York

First American Edition. Copyright © 1978
by Richard Scarry. All rights reserved under
International and Pan-American Copyright
Conventions. Published in the United
States by Random House, Inc., New York,
and simultaneously in Canada by Random
House of Canada Limited, Toronto. Origi-
nally published in Great Britain as *Richard
Scarry's Busy-busy Counting Book* by Wil-
liam Collins Sons & Co. Ltd., Glasgow and
London. Copyright © 1977 by William Col-
lins Sons & Co. Ltd. ISBN: 0-394-83966-8.
*Library of Congress Catalog Card
Number:* 78-55299.
Manufactured in the United States of
America   1 2 3 4 5 6 7 8 9 0

1 one

"What can I do today?" asks
Willy Bunny.
"Why don't you count all the things
you see?" says his father.
"That sounds like fun!"
cries Willy.
"I will start with me.
I am *one* bunny."

2 two

Oh, look! Here comes Sally Bunny. *One* bunny and *one* bunny make *two* bunnies. Both bunnies have *two* eyes, *two* hands, *two* feet . . .

. . . and *two* long ears.

3 three

Willy and Sally go outside to play.
Along comes their friend Freddy.
Two bunnies and *one* bunny make
three bunnies.

How many wheels are on Freddy's
tricycle? That's right! *Three*.

4 four

Here comes Flossie Bunny with her wagon. *Three* bunnies and *one* bunny make *four* bunnies.

Now there are *two* girl bunnies and *two* boy bunnies.

Flossie has brought *four* apples in her four-wheeled wagon. *One* for each bunny.

5 five

At the music school Willy meets the
tuba players. How many are there?
That's right! *Five.*
Oompah!
Oompah! Oompah!
Oompah! Oompah!

6 six

Willy sees Mother
Cat hanging her
washing on the
line. Oh, dear!
The shirts are
blowing away.
How many shirts?
Six.

7 seven

Willy watches *seven* cats running
past *seven* buckets.
Five young cats, a mother, and a baby
make *seven* cats.

8 eight

How many places are set at the table?
Eight.
There are *five* hot pies.
And *three* cold pies.
How many pies?
Eight.

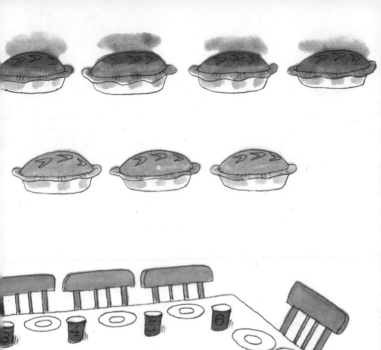

9 nine

There are *nine* hikers in the field.
Willy counts *four* sleeping . . .

. . . and *five* eating.

That makes *nine*.

Five trumpeters are playing, *tootle-tee-toot!*
Five drummers are drumming, *boom-boom!*

How many musicians
altogether?
That's right! *Ten*.

11 eleven

Eleven cats are playing soccer.
The goalkeeper is wearing
a green shirt.

How many are wearing blue?

12 twelve

Willy counts *twelve* hens.
Five of them are red.

Five of them are white.

And *two* are black.

13 thirteen

There are *thirteen* boats
out at sea.
Five are blue.
Five are red.
Three are yellow.

14 fourteen

Willy stops at Mr. Bug's flower shop. How many flowers does he count?

Four . . .

and *five* . . .

and *five* more.

That's right! *Fourteen.*

15 fifteen

There are *fifteen* airplanes at the Air Show.

Five have single wings.

Five have double wings.

Five have triple wings.

16 sixteen

Willy counts *sixteen* mouse cars.
My! What a bumpy road!
Eleven are falling off the carrier.

17 seventeen

Five submarines.

Willy is down at the beach.
He counts *seventeen* boats.

Five motorboats.

*(It looks
as if one
motorboat
is in
trouble.)*

Five rowboats.

And *two* police boats.

18 eighteen

Eighteen workers hurry home from work.

One of the workers is
Daddy Bunny.

Willy
is
greeting
him
at the
door.

19 nineteen

Willy sees *nineteen* frogs having
fun in the water.

How many
are floating?

How many are waving?

How many are swimming?

20 twenty

There are *twenty* carrots on the Bunny family's table. Willy has *five* all to himself. My, what a hungry bunny! Mmmm, those carrots taste good.

Willy Bunny has learned a lot about
counting.
I bet you have too.
See if you can add numbers the way
Willy has added them.
His Mommy and Daddy are very proud
of him.

1+1 = 2

2+1 = 3

2 + 2 = 4

3 + 2 = 5

3 + 3 = 6

---

4 + 3 = 7

4 + 4 = 8

5+4=9

5 + 5 = 10